# Not Just Pirates

*A Creative Graphic Novel to Boost English Skills for Young Middle School Learners (Grades 5-7) Includes Engaging, Fun-Filled Activities.*

## Emily Sherwood, PhD

*Special Gift For Parents and Children:*

**Does your child need extra help with English?**

**Looking for a fun way to boost their vocabulary and grammar?**

**Does your little one struggle with focus and learning and need one-on-one attention?**

**Scan the QR Code and Book a Free Call Right Now + Get a Free "Not Just Pirates" Audiobook.**

Interstate 26 South

It is my 13th birthday!

My name is Manuel. My Dad, Papa, said I could choose a place for my birthday...

I wanted to go to the beach...

My papa didn't like that...

Why don't we go to the mountains? They're closer.

We go there a lot! We never go to the beach!

Ok. We will go to the beach.

I can't wait!

Me either!

My dad is driving my friend Jayden and me to the beach this weekend.

1

The Beach, South Carolina

The hotel is weird.

What kind of place is this? Why are we staying here?

It was a good deal.

It's weirder inside.

Welcome to the Bonny Hotel!

Why is there so much pirate stuff here?

This hotel was built to honor Anne Bonny.

Who was she?

Anne Bonny was a pirate in the 1700s.

She stole things from other ships.

What happened to her?

A court in Jamaica said she should die.

Don't worry, they let her live because she was pregnant.

That is all we know. She disappeared. A story says her treasure is near here.

People have searched for her treasure, but none have found it.

The reviews didn't say anything about that.

Hurricane Season

What? What? What?

Don't worry. It looks sunny this weekend.

It's a great day for treasure hunting.

Treasure?

There is gold at Pirate Bay.

CAPT JAC

Many shipwrecks happened there.

I want to go there!

Me too!

Is that really a great idea?

The boys will love it.

Pirates were not good people.

Aww, it's just fun. No pirates live here.

It's my birthday weekend!

We can go for the afternoon. But we will return tonight.

State Road 77

This is in the middle of nowhere!

No, it's not.

It's 5 miles to Pirates Bay.

5 more miles! This road is terrible!

But it is a nice day…

Maybe not…

An hour later…

The rain stopped.

But the road is still wet…

We have to wait.

Can we go outside?

I guess so…

6

I lost my shoes.

It was too muddy.

And I lost my sunglasses!

But we don't need those. We need the compass!

It is almost dark.

We cannot see well. It is dangerous!

12

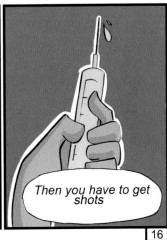

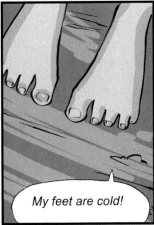

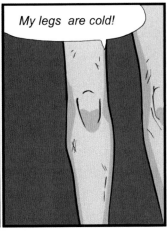

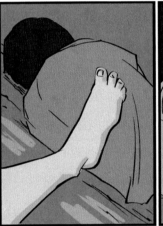

23

24

I found something!

What is it?
Is it a box?

It's not a box.
It's a chest

There is no lock.

Open it!

Oh.

# Fun Activities

# Level 1 (Beginner)
## Pirate Picture Puzzler: Find 5 Differences
### *Just a Little Warm-Up*

# Instructions:

Step 1 – Find 5 differences in 2 pictures and circle them using a pencil.

Step 2 – Write the differences you found below.

1 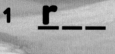 r _ _ _

2 m _ _

3 o _ _ _

4 b _ _ _ _

5 f _ _ _ _

# Level 2 (Beginner)
## Captain's Course:
## Navigate the Pirate Maze
### Uuuu... Be careful, don't get lost here. Find all 5!

# Instructions:

**Step 1 – Choose 1 of 2 entrances to find 5 missing items (Use a Pencil).**
**Step 2 – Check the box below once you find the item.**

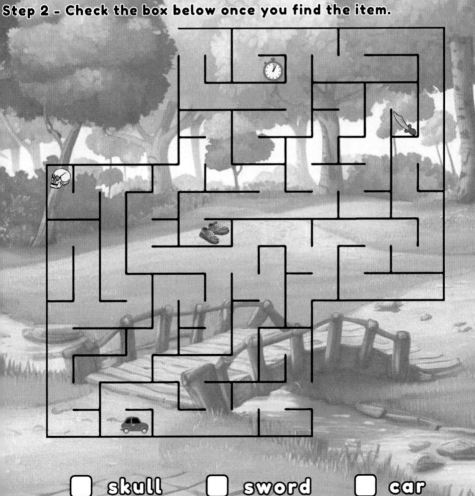

☐ skull   ☐ sword   ☐ car

☐ shoes   ☐ timer

# Level 3 (Intermediate) Buccaneer Word Search

## Now let's get more serious!

## Instructions:

Step 1 - Find and circle 11 words in the word search.

Step 2 - Write the word next to the correct picture.

| T | R | E | A | S | U | R | E | N | D | G | T |
|---|---|---|---|---|---|---|---|---|---|---|---|
| C | A | M | P | I | N | G | B | N | L | S | L |
| B | M | G | B | N | Y | G | E | E | E | W | C |
| O | A | Z | N | D | X | K | T | H | O | J | A |
| N | P | S | G | L | E | A | C | M | K | J | P |
| N | L | T | H | E | R | P | T | N | X | O | T |
| Y | K | Z | W | I | D | L | Z | P | T | R | A |
| T | Z | T | P | D | P | W | M | O | A | N | I |
| W | B | N | D | Q | Q | H | O | T | E | L | N |

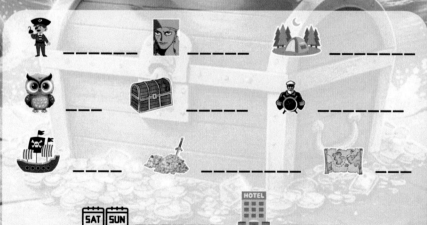

# Level 4 (Advanced)
## Pirate Perception Challenge: FInd 11 Differences
### Let's Level-Up Your Game!

# Instructions:

Step 1 - Find 11 differences in 2 pictures and circle them.
Step 2 - Write the differences you found below.

1  _ r _ _

2  b _ _ _ _

3  _ _ _ _ t

4  _ o _ _ _ _

5  _ _ x

6  f _ _ _

7  _ _ _ l _

8  _ _ _ _ _ _ e

9  p _ _ _ _ _ _

10  _ _ t

11  u _ _ _ _ _ _ _ _

# Level 5 (Expert)
## Pirate Vocabulary Voyage: Fill in the Blanks
### You can do it and nobody can stop you!

## Instructions:

**Step 1** - Write the correct word in each sentence(without looking at a story).
**Step 2** - Write the exact number of words you wrote in the box below.
**Step 3** - Go back and find the words you forgot and fill out the rest.

## Fill in the blanks

1. "I wanted to go to the _ _ _ _ _ ..."

2. "Anne Bonny was a _ _ _ _ _ _ in the 1700s."

3. "Maybe we can find a _ _ _ _ _ _ _ _ to help your family."

4. "It's _ _ _ _ _ _ _ inside."

5. "No. But I have a problem. I lost my _ _ _ _ _ ."

6. "The _ _ _ is rare. The chest is special too."

7. "It's _ _ _ _ _ '_ treasure!"

8. "We have a _ _ _ _ _ _ water."

9. "Jayden, you're _ _ _ _ _ _ _ _ !"

10. "My family was artists. We _ _ _ _ things."

☐ / ⑩

## In case you forgot:

1. Page 1   3. Page 24   5. Page 17   7. Page 9   9. Page 20

2. Page 3   4. Page 2   6. Page 29   8. Page 14   10. Page 22

# Level 6 (Mission-Impossible)
## Pirate Code Crossword: Crack the Story

*Now we are talking! Let's get focused, it's not going to be easy.*

# Instructions:

Step 1 - Answer 13 questions using a crossword.

Step 2 - Choose 4 words out of 13, click the button at the bottom of this page and write an interesting sentence(Pirate Related).

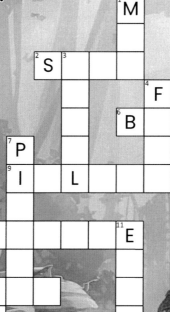

Crossword grid entries:
- 1. M
- 2. S — 3.
- 4. F
- 5. C
- 6. B
- 7. P
- 8. C
- 9. I — L
- 10. T
- 11. E
- 12. F
- 13. H

## Down

1. What do pirates use to find hidden treasure?
3. Where do pirates stay when they are not on their ship?
4. What do pirates eat to stay strong?
5. What do pirates put their treasure in?
7. Who sails the seas and looks for treasure?
11. What part of the body do pirates use to see?
13. What do pirates wear on their heads?

## Across

2. What do pirates use to travel across the ocean?
6. What do you call a young male pirate?
8. What do you call the group of people who work on a pirate ship?
9. Where do pirates often hide their treasure?
10. What are pirates always looking for that is full of gold and jewels?
12. What do you call the male parent of a young pirate?

Scan the QR Code and Add the Sentence

# WORD LIST

Find any word you desire!

| | | |
|---|---|---|
| Again | Another time | |
| Afternoon | 12:00 PM to 5:00 PM | |
| Art | Something handmade to look at (like paintings, weaving, drawings) | |
| Artist | Someone who makes art | |
| Bathroom | A room for washing | |
| Bay | Small area of water | |
| Beach | Land at an ocean | |
| Belt | A piece to wear on pants | |
| Birthday | Day of birth, day someone was born | |
| Boat | A vehicle for the water | |

| | | |
|---|---|---|
| Bottle | A tall container for liquids | |
| Book | Pages to be read together | |
| Box | Container with 4 sides | |
| Branches | Sticks on a tree | |
| Cafe | A place to eat and drink | |
| Camping | Living outside in nature | |
| Careful | Thinking about things before doing them | |
| Cold | At low temperature | |
| Court | Place where people are judged for crimes | |
| Creepy | Scary | |

| | | |
|---|---|---|
| Dad | A father | |
| Dark | Without light | |
| Deal | A good price | |
| Family | Group of people, for example: mothers and sons, grandmothers and grandchildren | |
| Feet | Body part under the legs | |
| Fire | Burning that makes it hot | |
| Food | What you eat | |
| Friend | Someone to spend time with | |
| Funny | Causing laughter | |
| Gold | A yellow metal | |

| | | |
|---|---|---|
| Ha ha | What is said when something is funny | |
| Head | Body part that has the face and brain | |
| Home | A place where someone lives | |
| Hotel | A place to stay when you are traveling | |
| Hour | 60 minutes | |
| Hungry | Wanting to eat | |
| Little | Small | |
| Lock | A barrier on a door or object | |
| Lucky | Fortunate, has good luck | |
| Lunch | The meal in the middle of the day | |

| | | |
|---|---|---|
| Map | A paper showing places | |
| Mean | Not nice | |
| Men | Teenage or adult boys | |
| Mile | 5,280 feet or 1.61 kilometers | |
| Minute | 60 seconds; there are 60 minutes in an hour | |
| Morning | The first part of the day, from around 5AM-12PM | |
| Mud | Soft, wet land | |
| Mushroom | A fungus that grows outside | |
| Owl | An animal that flies and lives at night | |
| Paper | Soft material to write or draw on | |

| | | |
|---|---|---|
| Pants | Long clothing worn on the legs | |
| Pirate | A person who steals from boats | |
| Place | A geographical point, like a building or area | |
| Poison | Something that can hurt or kill you | |
| Poor | Having little money | |
| Pregnant | Expecting a baby | |
| Problem | A trouble or issue | |
| Quickly | fast | |
| Quiet | Silent, not talking | |
| Rain | Water from the sky | |

| | | |
|---|---|---|
| Rat | A small animal that eats trash | |
| Return | Come back | |
| Rich | Having money | |
| Road | A place to drive cars and trucks | |
| Room | A space with walls and floors | |
| Sad | Not happy | |
| Safe | Not dangerous | |
| Sand | Yellow Land, often found at the beach | |
| Seaweed | A plant found in the ocean | |
| Ship | A big boat | |

| | | |
|---|---|---|
| Shipwrecks | Remains of ships | |
| Shorts | Short clothing worn on legs | |
| Shots | Injections | |
| Shower | A place to bathe with water from over you | |
| Silly | Not making sense, foolish | |
| Sleeping bag | A bag to sleep in outside | |
| Special | Unique, valuable | |
| Sticks | Pieces of wood on the ground | |
| Story | A telling of an event | |
| Tent | A shelter of cloth | |

| | | |
|---|---|---|
| Toilet | A place to sit in the bathroom | |
| Tomorrow | The day after today | |
| Too late | After the time when you can do something | |
| Tonight | The night of a morning or afternoon | |
| Trash | Waste, garbage | |
| Treasure | Things that cost a lot of money | |
| Underwear | Clothing wore under clothes | |
| United States | A country in North America | |
| War | A violent fight between 2 sides | |
| Water | Liquid, mostly clear | |

| | | |
|---|---|---|
| Weekend | Saturday and Sunday | |
| Wet | Covered with water | |
| Yuck | Gross! | |
| | | |
| | | |
| | | |
| | | |
| | | |
| | | |
| | | |

# ABOUT THE AUTHOR

## Dr. Emily Sherwood

Dr. Emily Sherwood, with her Ph.D. in Teacher Education from the University of Tennessee, has devoted nearly twenty years to literacy and English language education. Her expertise is evident in her teaching of students of all ages and diverse backgrounds across the United States. Her most impactful role was as a Reading Specialist at an English immersion school in Guangzhou, China, where she worked for three years, helping struggling and new readers thrive.

Currently, Emily lives in the picturesque Lowcountry of South Carolina, taking a break from traditional teaching to focus on her growing family. Her passion for education remains as strong as ever before, and she continues to inspire and support readers through her writing all around the world. Emily's work reflects her belief in the transformative power of reading, education, storytelling and visualization, making a lasting impact on everyone she reaches.

Made in the USA
Las Vegas, NV
11 December 2024

13955501R00033